ROLL ON

WRITTEN BY CONNIE TATE

ILLUSTRATED BY SAM BRIDGE

Lucky Jenny Publishing, Inc.
P.O. Box 331
Plymouth, CA 95669

For Wren,
who likes to carry her own load

It is Farmers' Market day and Wren is excited.

Every week Wren and her daddy visit Ms. Frieda's Fruit and Vegetable stand.

Ms. Frieda sells the most delicious fruits and vegetables.

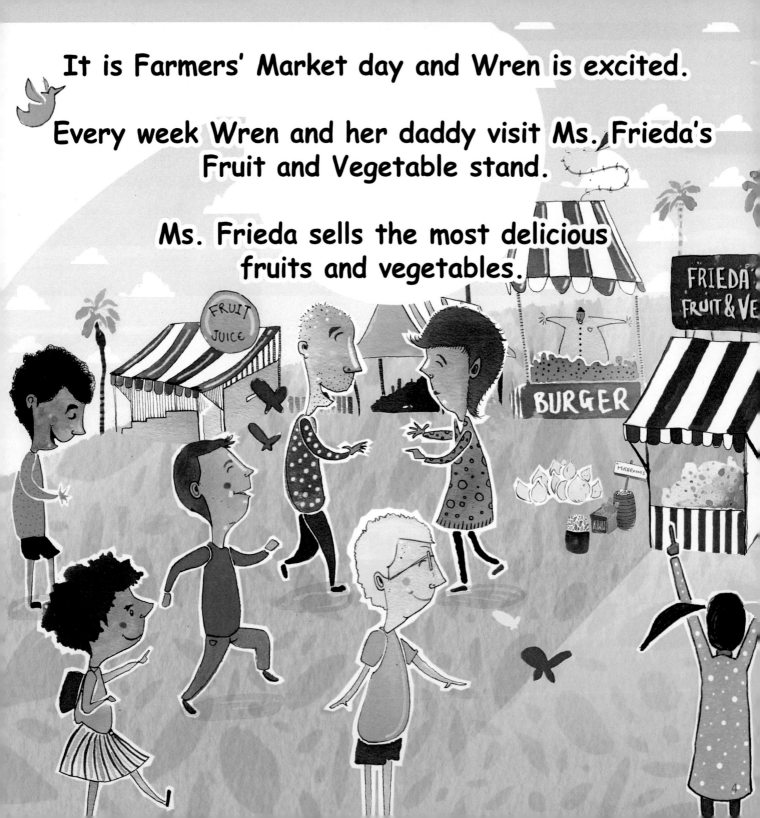

Wren loves to taste something new.

She has tasted exotic mushrooms, kiwi, jicama and sugar snap peas.

Wren wonders what Ms. Frieda will have today.

"Hello Ms. Frieda," says Wren.

"Hello Wren," says Ms. Frieda.

"Ms. Frieda, what do you recommend today?" asks Daddy.

"Today I have spaghetti squash."

Wren points to the biggest spaghetti squash.

"I want that one," says Wren.

Daddy smiles, buys the biggest spaghetti squash

and hands it to Wren.

Wren wraps her hands around the spaghetti squash,
but her arms are too short
and the spaghetti squash too heavy.

FRIEDA'S
FRUIT & VEG

Spaghetti squash tumbles to the ground and begins to roll.

"Stop!" yells Wren as spaghetti squash rolls into the street.

But spaghetti squash does not stop. Spaghetti squash rolls on.

Kaitlin drives past. Kaitlin sees spaghetti squash.

Kaitlin steps on the brakes!

"Stop!" yells Kaitlin as

spaghetti squash rolls under the car.

But spaghetti squash does not stop.
Spaghetti squash rolls on.

John walks his dog, Doogie.

John and Doogie

see spaghetti squash.

John runs right.

Doogie runs left.

"Stop!" yells John. "Woof!" barks Doogie.

Down go John and Doogie as

spaghetti squash rolls across the street.

But spaghetti squash

does not stop.

Spaghetti squash

rolls on.

WOOOOOOMPH!!

Cal rides his skateboard.

Cal sees spaghetti squash.

Cal flips his skateboard!

WHIZZZZZZ!!

"Stop!" yells Cal as spaghetti squash rolls around the skateboard.

But spaghetti squash does not stop. Spaghetti squash rolls on.

Tate and Teague wax their surfboards.

Tate and Teague see spaghetti squash.

Tate and Teague swing their surfboards!

"Stop!" yell Tate and Teague as

spaghetti squash rolls between the surfboards.

But spaghetti squash does not stop.
Spaghetti squash rolls on.

Spaghetti squash rolls and rolls.
"Stop!" everyone yells as spaghetti squash
rolls faster and faster.

But spaghetti squash does not stop.
Spaghetti squash rolls on. . .
down the hill, off the curb
and bounces high into the sky!

Squashed spaghetti squash!

Ms. Frieda reaches into her apron pocket and pulls out another spaghetti squash. Ms. Frieda winks and gently hands this spaghetti squash to Wren.

Wren wraps her hands around the spaghetti squash and this time her arms are not too short and the spaghetti squash not too heavy.

Connie Tate, Ed.D. has enjoyed a career in education for more than 40 years.

She resides with her husband Mick in Turlock, California. She has three adult daughters and ten grandchildren.

Her favorite quote is:

"There are lives I can imagine without children but none of them have the same laughter and noise." Brian Andreas

Sam Bridge is an illustrator living in London and New York. Graduating with a BA in Fine Art he is now drawing full time.

His work has been featured in exhibitions in London and America and he has also worked on children's books and editorials for The Guardian, Empire Online, Urban Outfitters and The English National Opera.

All his work in progress can be seen here:

www.sambridgeart.com

55112783R00015

Made in the USA
San Bernardino, CA
28 October 2017